Thomas Comes to Breakfast

The Rev. W Awdry

Illustrated by Clive Spong

KAYE & WARD · LONDON

Kaye & Ward
an imprint of William Heinemann Ltd
Michelin House
81 Fulham Road
London SW3 6RB

LONDON   MELBOURNE
AUCKLAND   JOHANNESBURG

First published 1985
Copyright © 1985 Kaye & Ward
First paperback edition 1987, reprinted 1987, 1988

ISBN 0 434 92755 4

Printed and bound in Great Britain by
William Clowes Limited, Beccles and London

Thomas the tank engine has worked his branch line for many years.
"You know just when to stop," laughed his Driver one day. "You could
almost manage without me."

Thomas didn't understand that his Driver was only joking.
"Driver says I don't need him any more," he told the others.

"Don't be so silly," said Percy.
"I'd never go without my Driver," said Toby earnestly. "I'd be frightened."

"Pooh!" boasted Thomas. "I'm not scared. Just you wait and see."

It was dark in the morning when the cleaner came to light the engines.
Thomas drowsed comfortably as the warmth spread through his boiler.

He woke again in daylight. Percy and Toby were still asleep.
"I'll give those silly 'stick-in-the-muds' a surprise," he chuckled.

He felt steam going first to one piston, and then to the other.
"I'm moving! I'm moving!" he whispered. "I'll creep outside and stop.
Then I'll wheesh loudly to make them jump."

Thomas thought he was clever, but really he was only moving because the careless cleaner had meddled with his controls. He tried to 'wheesh', but he couldn't. He tried to stop, but he couldn't. He just kept rolling along.

"Never mind, the buffers will stop me," he thought hopefully.
But that siding had no buffers. The rails ended at the road.

Thomas's wheels left the rails and crunched the tarmac. Ahead of him was a hedge, a garden gate and the Station-master's house.

The Station-master and his family were having breakfast. It was their favourite one of ham and eggs.

"Oh horrors!" exclaimed Thomas as he shut his eyes and plunged through the hedge.

No one came near him for a very long time – everyone was much too busy.
At last some workmen arrived to prop the house up with strong poles.

Next they brought a load of sleepers and made a road over the garden
so that . . .

. . . Donald and Douglas, puffing hard, could pull Thomas back to the rails again.

Thomas's funnel was bent. Bits of hedge, the garden gate and a broken
window-frame festooned his front end, which was badly twisted.

Thomas looked so comic that the twins laughed aloud. "Goodbye Thomas,"
they chuckled. "Don't forget your Driver next time!"

His Driver and Fireman began to tidy him up. "You're a perfect disgrace," they told him. "We're ashamed of you."

"And so am I," said a voice behind them. "You're a naughty engine."

"Yes, Sir, I'm sorry, Sir," faltered Thomas.

"You must go to the works to be mended, but they've no time for you now. Percy will take you to a siding where you can wait till they are ready."

Next day a diesel rail-car came. "Uuooo! Uuooo!" she tooted gaily, as she ran into the station.

The Fat Controller came over to Thomas. "That's Daisy," he said. "She's come to do your work. Diesels never run off to breakfast in Station-master's houses." And he walked sternly away.

Toby and Percy didn't like Daisy at first, they were afraid she might be troublesome.

"Please, Sir," they asked, "will she go when Thomas comes back?"

"That depends," said the Fat Controller.

Thomas didn't enjoy his time at the works. "It's nice to feel mended again," he said afterwards, "but they took so many of my old parts away and put new ones in, that I'm not sure whether I'm really me or another engine."

Meanwhile, as Toby and Percy had feared, Daisy was troublesome. She was fussy and lazy and got into difficulties with a bull . . .

When she said she was sorry Toby put in a good word for her and
the Fat Controller allowed her to stay after all.

Thomas, Percy, Toby and Daisy are now all good friends.
Thomas is glad to have Daisy's help with his passengers.
He is never now so silly as to think that he can manage without his Driver.